YOU ARE A

STAR!

Michael Parker

illustrated by Judith Rossell

Walker & Company New York

For Julia and Elena —All my love, Dad

To Isabel. You are a star! —J. R.

Originally published in Australia by HarperCollins Publishers Australia Pty Limited in 2010
First published in the United States of America in September 2012
by Walker Publishing Company, Inc., a division of Bloomsbury Publishing, Inc.
www.bloomsburykids.com

For information about permission to reproduce selections from this book, write to
Permissions, Walker BFYR, 175 Fifth Avenue, New York, New York 10010

Library of Congress Cataloging-in-Publication Data
Parker, Michael.
You are a star! / Michael Parker ; illustrations by Judith Rossell.
p.   cm.
Summary: A young girl takes a trip from her bedroom into the sky, past the moon,
and through the universe, learning that she is made of stars.
ISBN 978-0-8027-2841-8 (hardcover) • ISBN 978-0-8027-2842-5 (reinforced)
[1. Astronomy—Fiction. 2. Stars—Fiction. 3. Life (Biology)—Fiction.] I. Rossell, Judith, ill. II. Title.
PZ7.P22737Yo 2012   [E]—dc23   2011050073

Art created with acrylic paint, pen, pencil, rubber stamps, marbling, and vintage maps.
Typeset in Gill Facia
Book design by John Candell

Printed in China by Hung Hing Printing (China) Co., Ltd., Shenzhen, Guangdong
1 3 5 7 9 10 8 6 4 2 (hardcover)
1 3 5 7 9 10 8 6 4 2 (reinforced)

All papers used by Bloomsbury Publishing, Inc., are natural, recyclable products
made from wood grown in well-managed forests. The manufacturing processes
conform to the environmental regulations of the country of origin.

You are a star.

Not a movie star. Or a sports star.

You are a star from way, way up in the sky.

Look at the tip of your finger.

Just there.

Look at all the tiny grooves and curves.

Every little piece of that finger comes from way,

way up in the sky.

Come and see.

Up, up, up.

Past your bed,
past your window,
past your roof.

Up into the ink of the night.

It may be dark out here,

but the sky is not all empty and black.

Look. More stars than you can count

on all your fingers and all your toes.

Hundreds of stars.

Thousands.

Millions.

Just lie here for a while, with all the stars
above you and all the Earth below you.

Those stars over there are fires in the sky.

Giant fires a long, long way away.

Much, much hotter than a candle's flame.

Much, much farther away than our sun.

Let's have a closer look.

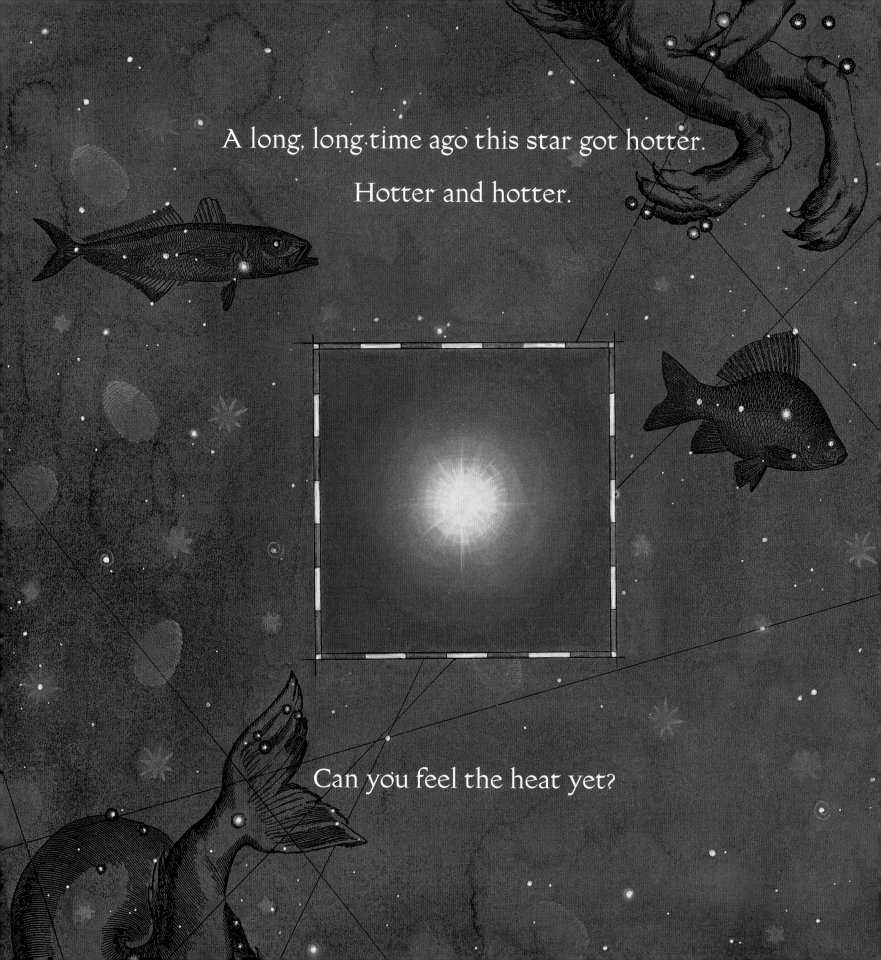

A long, long time ago this star got hotter.

Hotter and hotter.

Can you feel the heat yet?

Hotter and hotter

and hotter.

Until it exploded!

Are you okay?

Yes?

Good.

When the star exploded,

the tiny pieces flew across the sky.

Like lonely little boats.

Look at those tiny ones lit up

brighter than the rest.

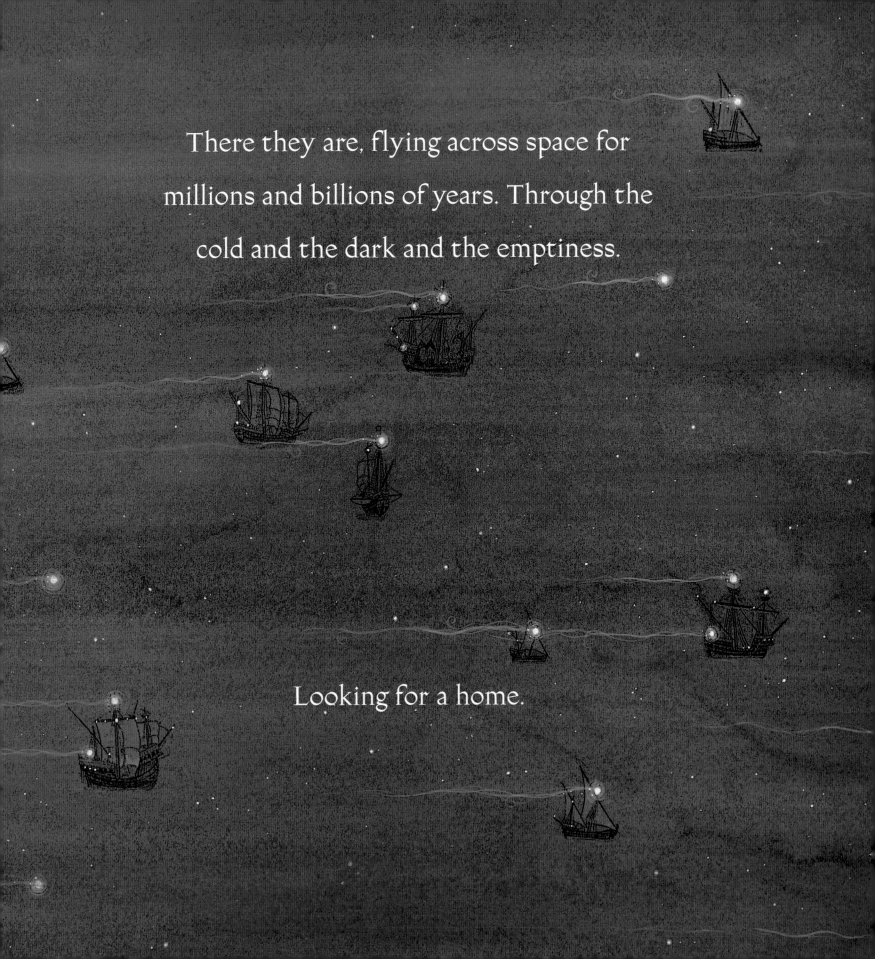

There they are, flying across space for millions and billions of years. Through the cold and the dark and the emptiness.

Looking for a home.

Until finally they come to rest in

the place that will be Earth.

And the place that will be Earth

tumbles and turns with our tiny

pieces of star inside.

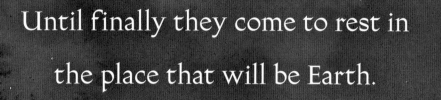

Look. Earth is getting

greener and cooler and more

beautiful as it turns.

And the tiny pieces of star

sail through rocks and plants

and fires.

Through animals and trees and fruit

until . . .

You eat the fruit, and then the tiny
pieces of star are inside you.

Sailing down through your mouth, your tummy,
your arm. Almost there. Until . . .

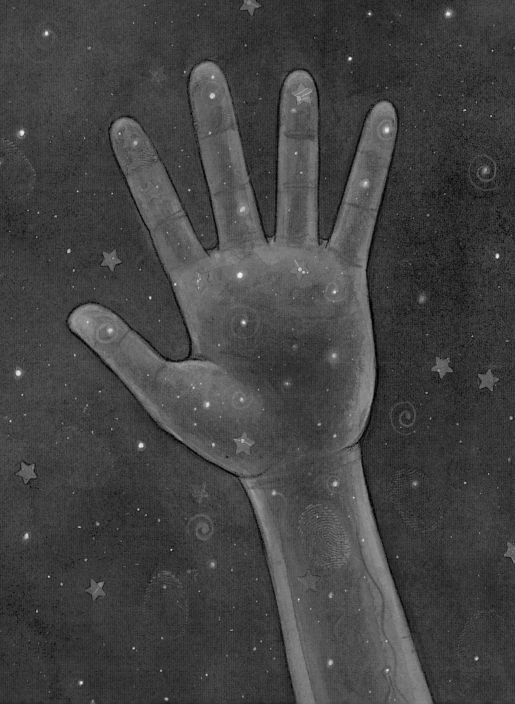

The tiny pieces of star are at the tip of your finger.

In among the grooves and curves.

Waving back at you.

It's time to return to your room.

Snuggle back into bed.

But remember, that sky way, way above

your bed is not cold and dark.

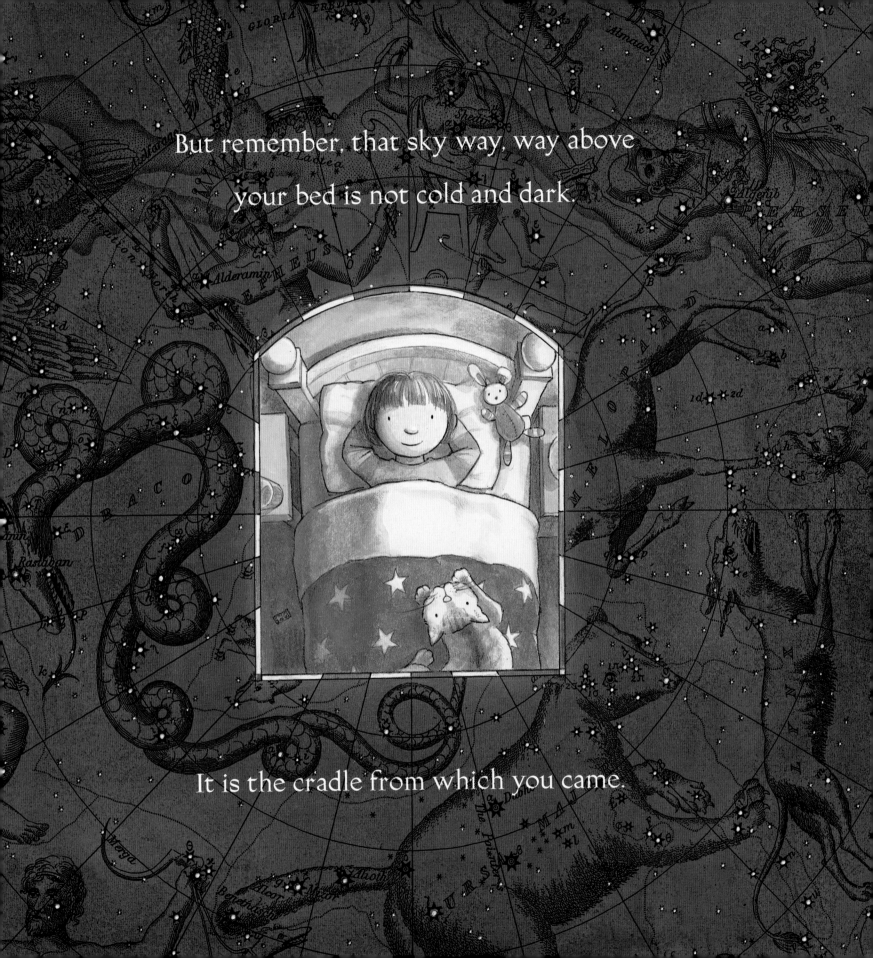

It is the cradle from which you came.

You are a star!

Star Facts

★ The sun, our closest star, is believed to be about 4.6 billion years old, about half its expected lifespan.

★ The amount of time a star lives is determined by its size. Smaller stars live billions of years, while larger stars live only millions of years because they burn out more quickly.

★ Stars come in many different colors. The hottest stars burn blue, medium-heat stars burn white or yellow, and the coldest stars burn red. Our sun burns yellow white.

★ The sun is part of the Milky Way galaxy, which is made up of billions of stars. Scientists believe there are billions of galaxies in the universe.

★ Some stars are so far away that by the time we see them twinkling in the night sky, their lights have already traveled for thousands of years just to reach Earth.

★ Stars look like they are twinkling because Earth's atmosphere warps their light rays.

★ The largest star known to humans is the "Pistol Star," and it is believed to be one hundred times the size of the sun and ten million times as bright. It is part of the Milky Way galaxy.

★ Many stars, called binary stars, come in pairs, and some even come in groups of three or four.

★ A "falling star" is not actually a star at all. It's a meteoroid, or dust and rock particles, falling through Earth's atmosphere and burning up.

★ A constellation is a map of stars used by astronomers to easily identify stars in the night sky. These star groups form familiar shapes, which were often turned into myths and legends by ancient civilizations in Greece, Rome, and Egypt, and by early Native Americans.